To Michel,
and all our Vespa rides through Paris.

To my parents,
who let me fly away to Paris.

Hélène

Translated from the French *Paris s'envole*

First published in the United Kingdom in 2015 by
Thames & Hudson Ltd, 181A High Holborn, London WC1V 7QX

www.thamesandhudson.com

First published in 2015 in hardcover in the United States of America by
Thames & Hudson Inc., 500 Fifth Avenue, New York, New York 10110

thamesandhudsonusa.com

Reprinted in 2016

British Library Cataloguing-in-Publication Data
A catalogue record for this book is available from the British Library

Library of Congress Catalog Card Number 2015937879

ISBN 978-0-500-65059-2

Printed in China in July-August 2016 by
Toppan Leefung, Dongguang City, Guangdong Province.

PARIS
Up, Up and Away

Thames & Hudson

Hélène Druvert

The Eiffel Tower is bored today.
Wouldn't it be nice to fly away?
Paris is full of things to do.
The Tower would like to see them too.

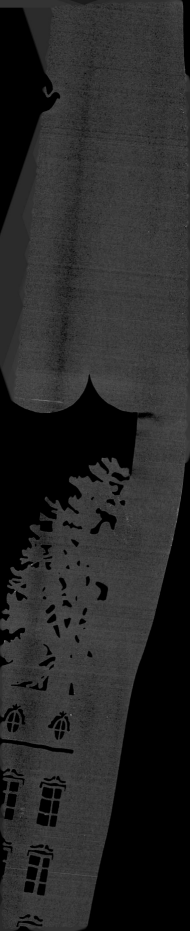

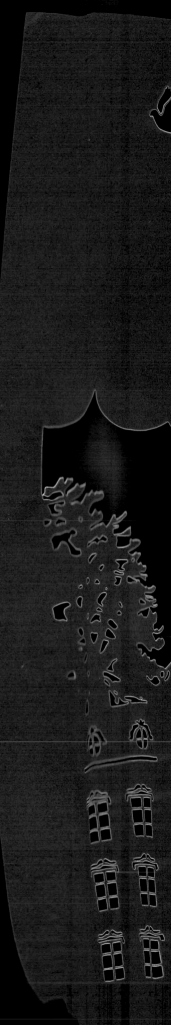

The Tower takes
off for the day
To watch the city
work and play...

The Tower looks down from the sky
And sees the River Seine roll by.

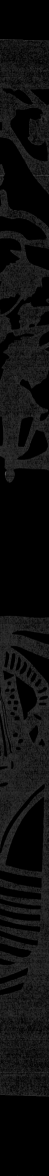

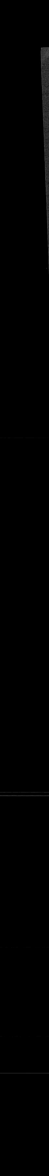

It passes the bridges and boats below
But the clouds are turning dark – oh no!

The Opéra is the Tower's next stop
Where ballerinas twirl and hop.

The Tower shrinks down small and neat
To walk with people on the street.

It visits a big department store

With lovely things on every floor.

The sun comes
out and the
sky is clear.
The Tower
lands in
a park
that's near.

While the children play and the birds fly free,
The Tower snoozes under a tree.

The Tower wakes up.

Is someone calling?

The Notre-Dame bells say night is falling!

The Tower switches on its lights
And shines them on the city's sights.

Goodnight Paris! The day is done
But I'm sure tomorrow will bring more fun!